THIS BLOOMSBURY BOOK

BELONGS TO

....

To Erin ~ MN

For Luba & Manja ~ KWM

First published in Great Britain in 2005 by Bloomsbury Publishing Plc
36 Soho Square, London, W1D 3QY
This revised paperback edition first published in 2008

A CIP catalogue record of this book is available from the
British Library
ISBN 978 0 7475 6426 3
Printed in Belgium by Proost
3 5 7 9 10 8 6 4 2
All papers used by Bloomsbury Publishing are natural,
recyclable products made from wood grown in
well-managed forests. The manufacturing processes
conform to the environmental regulations of the
country of origin

Marjorie Newman

Pictures by

Ken Wilson-Max

Tom was going to have a new baby brother or sister. There was a lot to do getting everything ready. Dad got the cot down from the loft.

'That's my cot!' said Tom.

'You've got a big bed now,' said Dad.

One evening Granny came to stay while Mum and Dad went off to the hospital.

'You'll soon be able to see the baby!' Granny told Tom.

Next day Dad took
Tom and Gran to
the hospital.
'It's a boy!' Dad
told Tom, proudly.
Tom looked at
the baby.
It was not pretty.

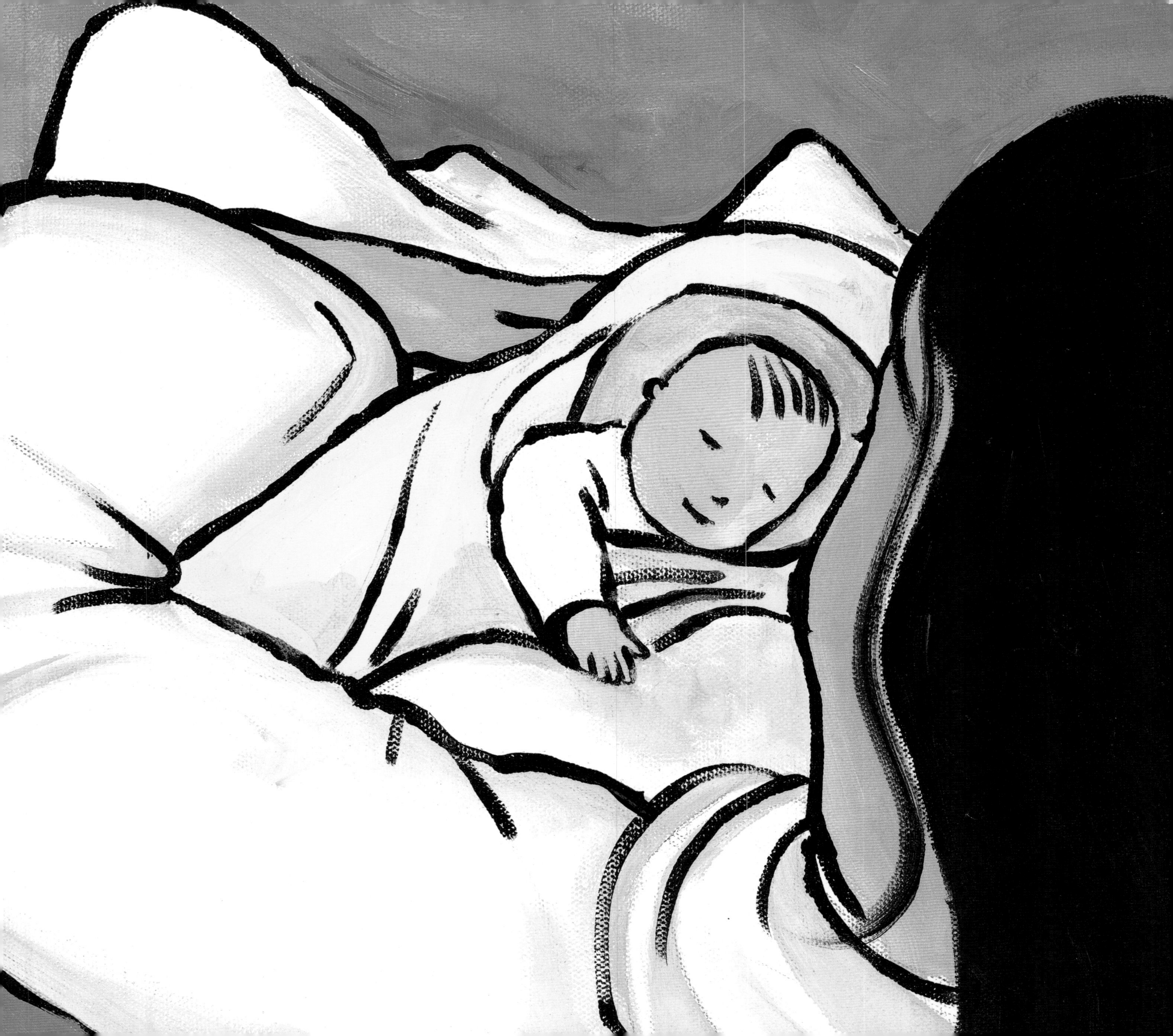

Soon Mum and Dad brought the baby home.

Lots of visitors came.

They brought presents for Tom and the baby.

'He's a gorgeous baby!' everyone said.

'Coochy coochy coo!' they chorused.

Tom watched.

The baby was a lot of work.

Mum bathed it.

Mum fed it.

Dad changed its nappy.

Dad tidied away its things.

Tom watched.

'Wouldn't you like to help?' asked Mum.

'No,' said Tom.

The baby cried a lot.

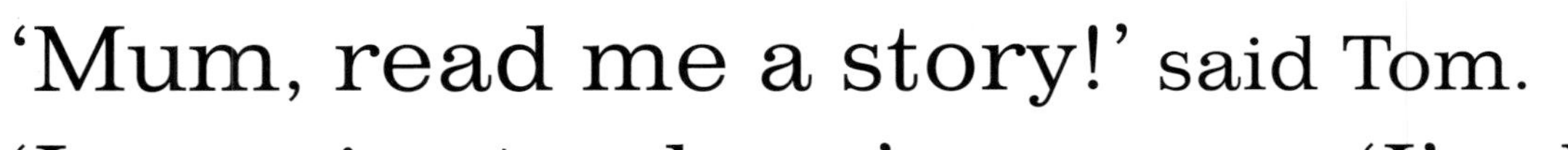

'Mum, read me a story!' said Tom.
'In a minute, dear,' said Mum. 'I'm busy with the baby.'
'I want to go to the park!' announced Tom.
'Presently,' said Mum.
'Let's play hide and seek!' suggested Tom.
'Tom, could you be a good boy and hand me the baby's towel?' Mum asked.

'No!' yelled Tom. 'No!

No!

No!'

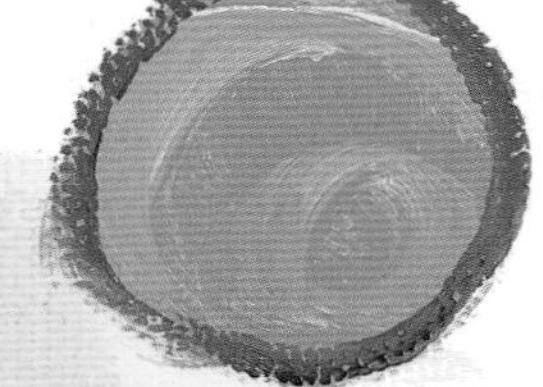

He picked up the towel.
He threw it
across the room.

'I hate that baby!' yelled Tom.

Tom rushed upstairs
and into the baby's
room.
He climbed into
the cot. Dad came
running up the stairs.

‘Hey, hey, hey!’ he said. ‘What’s all this about?’
‘It’s my cot!’ sobbed Tom.
‘I want my cot! I want my mum!’

Mum cuddled Tom while Dad got out a photograph album. He sat beside Mum and Tom. 'Look, Tom!' he said.

'That's him in my cot!' yelled Tom.

'No,' said Mum.

'That's you in your cot when you were a baby.'

Dad showed Tom some photographs.

'That's you, too,' said Mum, 'learning to walk.'

'This baby will grow and stop crying so much, Tom. Just like you did,' said Dad.

'He'll stop needing me so much,' said Mum.

'Just like you did.'

‘He’ll even grow out of the cot and need a big bed,’ smiled Mum.

‘Just like you did,’ said Dad.

Tom went to look at the baby. The baby looked up at Tom.
Then Tom said, ‘I’m hungry.’

'Let's all have sausages and chips,' said Mum.
'Not the baby?' said Tom.
'Good gracious me, no,' said Mum and Dad together.
'He's much too small.'
'One day he'll grow,' said Tom. 'Just like I did.'
'We can't go back to the way things were, Tom,' said Dad.
'We have to keep going on to new things…
Just like you did.'

At bedtime, Mum and Dad tucked Tom into bed. They tucked his new cuddly toys in beside him.

'It's a good job it's a big bed,' said Tom, sleepily.

He liked his new cuddly toys. But most of all he cuddled his old teddy bear into his arms because the old teddy bear had come first, and was special.